FREDERICK WARNE

Published by the Penguin Group
27 Wrights Lane, London W8 5TZ, England
Penguin Books USA Inc., 375 Hudson Street, New York, New York 10014, USA
Penguin Books Australia Ltd, Ringwood, Victoria, Australia
Penguin Books Canada Ltd, 10 Alcorn Avenue, Toronto, Ontario, Canada M4V 3B2
Penguin Books (N.Z.) Ltd, 182-190 Wairau Road, Auckland 10, New Zealand

Penguin Books Ltd, Registered Offices: Harmondsworth, Middlesex, England

First published 1996 by Frederick Warne
5 7 9 10 8 6 4

ISBN 0 7232 4327 1

Printed and bound in Great Britain by
William Clowes Limited, Beccles and London

A First Peter Rabbit Book

A LEARNING BOOK FOR YOUNG CHILDREN

Meet Peter Rabbit

This is naughty Peter Rabbit.
He squeezes under Mr. McGregor's
garden gate to eat lettuces.
Mr McGregor chases poor
Peter all over the
garden and he
only just
escapes,
leaving his
jacket and shoes
behind him.

Here are some of
Peter's friends.

Jemima Puddle-Duck

Benjamin Bunny

Tom Kitten

Mrs Tiggy-Winkle

Mr Jeremy Fisher

Mrs Tittlemouse

Farmyard noises

Peter and Benjamin can see Mr McGregor's cat. She says *Miaow Miaow*.

Listen to the noises the animals make.

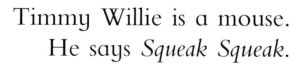

Timmy Willie is a mouse. He says *Squeak Squeak*.

Here are the Puddle-ducks. They say *Quack Quack*.

Sally Henny-Penny is a speckled hen. She says *Cluck Cluck*.

This is Kep the sheepdog with Jemima. He says *Woof Woof*.

Aunt Pettitoes has eight noisy piglets. They grunt *Oink Oink*.

Can you make all of these sounds?

Happy families

Peter Rabbit has three **sisters** called Flopsy, Mopsy, and Cotton-tail. They live with their **mother**, old Mrs Rabbit.

Meet some more families.

This is Pigling Bland walking with his **brother**, Alexander.

Here is Hunca Munca
with her **babies**.

Here are the Flopsy Bunnies.
Their **mother** is Peter's **sister**,
Flopsy and their **father**
is Peter's **cousin**,
Benjamin Bunny.

Mrs Tabitha Twitchit has two
daughters called Mittens and
Moppet and one naughty **son**
called Tom.

Animal friends

Peter Rabbit and Benjamin Bunny are friends. They have many exciting adventures together, usually in Mr McGregor's garden!

Meet some more friends.

Johnny Town-mouse is drinking a glass of milk with his country friend, Timmy Willie.

Kep the sheepdog lets his friend, Jemima, out of the shed.

Lucie helps her friend, Mrs Tiggy-winkle, down the hill.

Mr Jeremy Fisher is telling his friend about his fishing trip.

Mrs Tittlemouse has invited five friends to her party.

Who is your best friend?

Animal houses

Peter Rabbit lives with his mother and sisters in a sand-bank underneath the root of a very big fir-tree. His home is called a burrow

Look at the houses of Peter' friends.

Squirrel Nutkin lives with his cousins in a wood at the edge of a lake.

Old Brown the owl lives on an island in the middle of a lake. He is flying back to his house in the hollow of an oak-tree. Can you see the little brown door?

Jemima Puddle-duck lives on the farmyard with the chickens and cows.

Hunca Munca and Tom Thumb live in a mouse-hole under the skirting board. Here they are peeking out!

Mr Jeremy Fisher lives in a little damp house at the edge of a pond. His house is full of water but he likes it that way!

Timmy Willie loves his peaceful burrow in a country garden, where he can smell violets and spring grass.

Mrs Tiggy-winkle has just locked the door to her little house on a hill. Can you see where she is hiding the key?

Poor Tom Kitten has fallen right into Samuel Whisker's dirty home in the attic.

Mrs Tittlemouse lives in a funny little house under a hedge. It is full of sandy passages leading to storerooms and nut-cellars.

This old woman mouse lives in a shoe with all her children. That must be the strangest house of all!

Where do you live?

At home

Here is Peter's mother, old Mrs Rabbit, cooking in the burrow **kitchen**. She is wondering what Peter has done with his clothes! Can you see the pans hanging on the wall?

The two bad mice are in the dolls' **bedroom.** Hunca Munca is pulling out the feathers from the pillow.

The cat is in the **living room**. She is looking for mice under the sofa pillow.

Ribby is warming herself by the **fireplace**. Can you see the kettle hanging over the fire?

Timmy Willie has joined a mouse dinner-party in the **dining room**.

Samuel Whiskers is running up the **staircase**. He has just stolen some butter.

Playtime

Peter Rabbit is having fun in Mr. McGregor's garden, eating his lettuces and radishes.

What games do Peter's friends like to play?

Look at the kittens playing in the garden. Their clean clothes will soon be dirty again!

Squirrel Nutkin is playing games when he ought to be gathering nuts.

These rabbits are dancing to pipe music. How many dancing rabbits can you count?

Miss Moppet is peeking through a hole in the handkerchief. She thinks the mouse can't see her.

What is your favourite game?

Keeping clean and tidy

Mrs Tiggy-winkle the washer-woman has washed Peter's blue jacket and Benjamin's red handkerchief. She is always very busy washing and ironing the animals' clothes.

What does she do with her washing?

Mrs Tiggy-winkle collects
the dirty clothes in a
laundry-basket.

She puts the socks into
pairs. These belong to
Sally Henny-Penny.

She hangs the clothes on a
clothes-line to air. She must
stand on her tiptoes to reach.

When the clothes are dry,
Mrs Tiggy-winkle irons the
creases out.

"Shoo! Shoo!" she says to the beetle.

Mrs Tittlemouse is a terribly tidy mouse. She won't allow anyone to leave dirty footprints in her house and is always sweeping and dusting the floors.

She mops the floor after Mr Jackson.

She polishes her little tin spoons.

Then, Mrs Tittlemouse is s tired, she falls fast asleep.

Tabitha Twitchit is having a tea party so she fetches the kittens indoors to wash and dress them before her friends arrive.

First she scrubs their faces.

Then she brushes their fur.

Then Tabitha combs their tails and whiskers. The kittens are ready to be dressed.

Now, those naughty kittens are in a mess again. Their mother will be furious!

Getting dressed

Wearing clothes helps to keep you warm and dry and makes you look nice. Old Mrs Rabbit makes sure that Peter keeps warm by doing up the buttons on his little blue jacket.

Aunt Pettitoes ties Pigling Bland's scarf to make him tidy for market.

Tabitha is going to dress
Tom in his best blue suit.

Oh dear! Tom is very fat and
several buttons have burst off.

The guinea-pig is tying
his beautiful bow-tie.

Doesn't he look fine in
his jacket and hat?

What do you like to wear?

Getting about

Poor Peter Rabbit is being chased by
Mr McGregor. He is **hopping** as fast as
he can, all the way home.

The Puddle-ducks are **walking** up
the road, keeping step - pit pat,
paddle pat! pit pat, waddle pat!

Jemima Puddle-duck is **flying** over the wood looking for a place to build her nest.

Mr Jeremy Fisher is **swimming** to the edge of the pond.

Hunca Munca and Tom Thumb are **running** back to their mouse-hole.

Benjamin Bunny sets off with a **hop**, **skip** and a **jump** to call on Peter Rabbit.

Going visiting

Peter Rabbit decides to visit Mr McGregor's vegetable garden, though Mr McGregor is not at all pleased to see him!

Who else is going visiting?

Hunca Munca and Tom Thumb visit the dolls' house when the dolls are out.

Lucie is a polite visitor. She knocks on Mrs Tiggy-winkle's front door before coming in.

Mrs Tabitha Twitchit has invited her friends to a tea party.

The squirrels bring a new-laid egg in a little basket as a present for Old Brown. They would like to gather nuts on his island.

Ribby knocks on the front door. She has come to visit Tabitha.

Johnny Town-mouse is visiting Timmy Willie. He has brought his suitcase for a long stay.

Who is this knocking at Cotton-tail's door?

It's a little black rabbit with a present of carrots!

Here is a red ladybird running up the passage.

Poor Mrs Tittlemouse always has plenty of visitors in her house but they come in without any invitation!

Here is Mr Jackson, in front of the fire!

Here is Babbitty Bumble, who came in at a window.

Here are some guests that Mrs Tittlemouse did invite!

Shopping

Ginger and Pickles own the village shop. Ginger is a yellow tom cat and Pickles is a little dog. Their shop is very popular with Peter Rabbit and his friends.

What do you think Peter is going in to buy?

These kittens are looking through the shop window at the jars of toffee.

Ginger and Pickles are behind the shop counter. The rabbits are waiting to be served.

Mrs Tiggy-winkle buys some soap and puts it into her shopping bag.

The customers at Ginger and Pickles' shop come in crowds every day. Sometimes they stop to talk outside the shop.

Cooking

Old Mrs Rabbit is making some camomile tea for Peter Rabbit, because he is too ill to eat. She boils the water in the kettle and brings him a cup of tea in bed.

Ribby has made a delicious mouse pie. She is putting it into the oven to bake it.

This little pig is peeling apples for an apple pie.

Mrs Tiggy-winkle has made some tea for herself and Lucie.

This pig is peeling potatoes and putting them in a saucepan.

The pussy-cat is toasting a bun
over the fire. She has invited a little
dog for tea.

Can you see the kettle by the fire?

Cecily Parsley is brewing cowslip
wine for the visitors who
come to her inn.

What colour is her apron?

Dinnertime

Peter is too ill to eat
his supper but his
sisters have bread and
milk and blackberries
for dinner.

Old Brown is eating his honey.
But Nutkin disturbs his dinner by
peeking in through the door
and singing a riddle.

A beautiful dinner is laid out upon the table but Hunca Munca and Tom Thumb don't know that the food isn't real. What a disappointment!

Mrs Tittlemouse offers Mr Jackson cherry-stones for dinner, but he cannot eat them because he has no teeth.

Next, she offers him thistle-down seed, but Mr Jackson would like some honey instead!

Timmy Willie has never been to a mouse dinner-party before. He is so nervous that he drops his plate!

Johnny Town-mouse has come to visit Timmy Willie in the country. They are eating herb pudding.

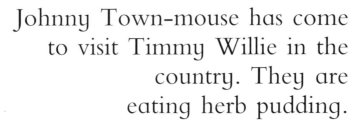

Pigling Bland is eating a bowl of oatmeal porridge before the fire. Pig-wig would like some too.

Tom Kitten is being rolled
into a kitten dumpling!
But the nasty rats are scared
away and have to leave
the pudding behind.

Ribby eats hot buttered muffins
with tea but she has cooked
Duchess a delicious mouse pie.

Mr Jeremy Fisher is sitting
down to dinner with his
friends. They are eating
a roast grasshopper.

What would you like to eat for your dinner?

Bedtime

Peter Rabbit has been put to bed because he is feeling sick. His mother has brought him a cup of camomile tea to make him feel better but Peter does not want to drink it!

Timmy Willie climbs into the vegetable hamper and falls fast asleep in a pea-pod.